CW00943451

POETRY & PROSE
for Cat Lovers

Cats: Poetry & Prose

The smallest feline is a masterpiece.

Leonardo da Vinci

When I play with my cat, who knows
whether she is now amusing herself with me
more than I with her?

Michel de Montaigne

Cats: Poetry & Prose

Our perfect companions never have fewer than four feet.

Colette

Cats seem to go on the principle that it never does any harm to ask for what you want.

Joseph Wood Krutch

Cats: Poetry & Prose

Stately, kindly, lordly friend,
Condescend
Here to sit by me, and turn
Glorious eyes that smile and burn,
Golden eyes, love's lustrous meed,
On the golden page I read.

All your wondrous wealth of hair,
Dark and fair,
Silken-shaggy, soft and bright
As the clouds and beams of night,
Pays my reverent hand's caress
Back with friendlier gentleness.

Algernon Swinburne, To a Cat

Cats: Poetry & Prose

Cats are a mysterious kind o' folk.
There is more passing in their minds than
we are aware of.

Sir Walter Scott

I can say with sincerity that I like cats . . .
A cat is an animal which has more human
feelings than almost every other.

Emily Bronte

Cats: Poetry & Prose

O bard-like spirit! beautiful and swift!
Sweet lover of the pale night;
The dazzling glory of the gold-tinged tail,
Thy whisker-wavering lips!

Percy Bysshe Shelley

Cats: Poetry & Prose

"All right," said the Cat.
And this time it vanished quite slowly,
beginning with the end of the tail, and ending
with the grin, which remained some time
after the rest of it had gone.

"Well! I've often seen a cat without a grin,"
thought Alice; "but a grin without a cat!
It's the most curious thing I ever saw
in all my life!"

Lewis Carroll, Alice in Wonderland

Cats: Poetry & Prose

Cruel, but composed and bland,
Dumb inscrutable and grand,
So Tiberius might have sat,
Had Tiberius been a cat.

Matthew Arnold, Poor Mathias

Cats: Poetry & Prose

I respect cats, they seem to have so much
else in their heads besides their mess.

Ralph Waldo Emerson

No matter how much cats fight,
there always seem to be plenty of kittens.

Abraham Lincoln

Cats: Poetry & Prose

The Owl and the Pussy-cat went to sea,
In a beautiful pea-green boat.
They took some honey and plenty of money
Wrapped up in a five-pound note.
The owl looked up to the stars above,
And sang to a small guitar,
'O lovely Pussy! O Pussy my love,
What a beautiful Pussy you are, you are,
What a beautiful Pussy you are!'

Edward Lear

Cats: Poetry & Prose

Female cats are very lascivious, and make advances to the male.

Aristotle

If stretching were wealth, the cat would be rich.

African Proverb

Cats: Poetry & Prose

The cat of the slums and alleys, starved, outcast, harried, still keeps amid the prowlings of its adversity the bold, free, panther-tread with which it paced of yore the temple courts of Thebes, still displays the self-reliant watchfulness which man has never taught it to lay aside.

Saki

Cats: Poetry & Prose

Within that porch, across the way
I see two naked eyes this night
Two eyes that neither shut nor blink
Searching my face with a green light
But cats to me are strange, so strange
I cannot sleep if one is near
And though I'm sure I see those eyes
I'm not so sure a body's there!

W H Davies, The Cat

Cats: Poetry & Prose

At Aix-en-Provence on the festival of Corpus Christi the finest tom-cat in the country, wrapped like a child in swaddling clothes, was publicly exhibited in a magnificent shrine.

Every knee was bent, every hand strewed flowers or poured incense, and in short the cat on this occasion was treated like the god of the day.

C Mills

Cats: Poetry & Prose

Curiosity killed the cat,
Satisfaction brought it back!

English Proverb

They say the text of literary power is
whether a man can write an inscription.
I say, 'Can he name a kitten?'

Samuel Butler

Cats: Poetry & Prose

You have now learned to see
That cats are much like you and me
And other people whom we find
Possessed of various types of mind.

T S Eliot

Cats: Poetry & Prose

At times half a dozen or more cats lived together under our roof; for, having a kindly feeling towards dumb animals, stray cats always received at our hands a hearty welcome, and were at once admitted to nursery, parlour, or kitchen.

We have said truly that each lived to purpose: for now one would purr by the sick child's pillow, lulling him to sleep with a low, soft song; then another would emerge triumphantly from the neighbourhood of the larder, bearing the fierce rat whose depredations had been for weeks the theme of household lamentation; and a third would allow a group of little children to amuse

Cats: Poetry & Prose

themselves at its expense for hours in
succession, permitting them to hug it and lug
it about, tug at its ears, and turn them inside
out, dress it up, almost squeeze the breath
out of its body — aye, and even hold it up by
the tail with never a complaint, save that
expressed in an occasional involuntary mew.

Mrs. Surr, Pets and Playfellows

Cats: Poetry & Prose

Another cat? Perhaps.

For love there is also a season; its seed must be resown. But a family cat is not replaceable like a wornout coat or set of tires. Each new kitten becomes its own cat, and none is repeated. I am four cats old, measuring out my life in friends that have succeeded but not replaced one another.

Irving Townsend

Cats: Poetry & Prose

A cat's rage is beautiful, burning with pure cat flame, all its hair standing up and crackling blue sparks, eyes blazing and sputtering.

William S Burroughs

The cat is a good friend, only she scratches.

Portuguese Proverb

Cats: Poetry & Prose

The trouble with cats is that they've got no tact.

P G Wodehouse

The Cat only grinned when it saw Alice.

It looked good-natured, she thought: still it had very long claws and a great many teeth, so she felt it ought to be treated with respect.

Lewis Carroll, Alice in Wonderland

Cats: Poetry & Prose

Cat said,
'I am not a friend and I am not a servant.
I am the Cat who walks by himself.'

Rudyard Kipling, The Cat that Walked by Himself, from the Just So Stories

Cats are living adornments.

Edwin Lent

Cats: Poetry & Prose

Here lies Richard Whittington, thrice mayor,
and his dear wife, a virtuous loving pair.
Him fortune raised to be beloved and great,
By the adventure only of a cat.

Epitaph from Richard Whittington's tomb

Cats: Poetry & Prose

Cats, no less liquid than their shadows,
Offer no angles to the wind.
They slip, diminished, neat, through
    loopholes
Less than themselves; will not be pinned.

To rules or routes for journeys; counter
Attack with non-resistance; twist
Enticing through the curving fingers
And leave an angered, empty fist.

They wait, obsequious as darkness
Quick to return, quick to return;
Admit no aim or ethics; flatter
With reservations; will not learn

Cats: Poetry & Prose

To answer to their names; are seldom
Truly owned till shot and skinned.
Cats, no less liquid than their shadows,
Offer no angles to the wind.

A S J Tessimond,
Cats no less Liquid than their Shadows

Cats: Poetry & Prose

The cat has nine lives–
    three for playing,
    three for straying,
    three for staying.

Anon

Curiosity killed the cat.

Traditional

Cats: Poetry & Prose

We have a black cat and an old dog at the
Rectory. I know somebody to whose knee
that black cat loves to climb; against whose
shoulder and cheeks it likes to purr ...

And what does that somebody do?
He quietly strokes the cat, and lets her sit.

Charlotte Brontë

Cats: Poetry & Prose

Cat mighty dignified till de dog come by.

American Negro Proverb

The cat is the only non-gregarious domestic
animal. It is retained by its extraordinary
adhesion to the comforts of the house in
which it is reared.

Francis Galton

Cats: Poetry & Prose

Dear creature by the fire a-purr,
Strange idol eminently bland,
Miraculous puss! As o'er your furr
I trail a negligible hand

And gaze into your gazing eyes,
And wonder in a demi-dream
What mystery it is that lies
Behind those slits that glare and gleam.

Lytton Strachley

Cats: Poetry & Prose

Her conscious tail her joy declared.

Thomas Gray,
Ode on the Death of a Favourite Cat

What astonished him was that cats should have two holes cut in their coats exactly at the places where their eyes were.

G C Lichtenbert

Cats: Poetry & Prose

The only subject on which Montmorency and I have any serious difference of opinion is cats. I like cats; Montmorency does not.

Jerome K Jerome

Cat: n. A soft, indestructible automaton provided by nature to be kicked when things go wrong in the domestic circle.

Ambrose Bierce

Cats: Poetry & Prose

The cat went here and there
And the moon spun round like a top,
And the nearest kin of the moon,
The creeping cat, looked up.
Black Minnaloushe stared at the moon,
For, wander and wail as he would,
The pure cold light in the sky
Troubled his animal blood.
Minnaloushe runs in the grass
Lifting his delicate feet.
Do you dance, Minnaloushe, do you dance?
When two close kindred meet,
What better than call a dance?
Maybe the moon may learn
Tired of that courtly fashion,

Cats: Poetry & Prose

A new dance turn.
Minnaloushe creeps through the grass
From moonlit place to place,
The sacred moon overhead
Has taken a new phase.
Does Minnaloushe know that his pupils
Will pass from change to change,
And that from round to crescent,
From crescent to round they range?
Minnaloushe creeps through the grass
Alone, important and wise,
And lifts to the changing moon
His changing eyes.

W B Yeats, The Cat and The Moon

Cats: Poetry & Prose

The hapless nymph with wonder saw,
A whisker first and then a claw.
With many an ardent wish,
She stretched in vain to reach the prize.
What female heart can gold despise,
What Cat's averse to fish?

*Thomas Gray, Ode on the Death of a
Favourite Cat*

Cats: Poetry & Prose

Careful observers may foretell the hour,
By sure prognostics when to dread a shower;
While rain depends, the pensive cat gives
    o'er,
Her frolics, and pursues her tail no more.

Jonathan Swift

Cats: Poetry & Prose

Learn we might, if not too proud to stoop
To quadruped instructors, many a good
And useful quality, and virtue too,
Rarely exemplified among ourselves,—
Attachment never to be weaned or changed
By any change of fortune, proof alike
Against unkindness, absence, and neglect.

Cowper

Cats: Poetry & Prose

Macavity, Macavity, there's no one like
    Macavity,
There never was a Cat of such deceitfulness
    and suavity.
He always has an alibi, and one or two to
    spare:
At whatever time the deed took place—
    Macavity wasn't there!

T S Eliot, Macavity: The Mystery Cat

Cats: Poetry & Prose

There was never a time when our household did not have several cats and they all had their particular charm. Their innate grace and daintiness, and their deeply responsive affection made them all dear to me.

James Herriot

Cats: Poetry & Prose

One evening, after a year's absence, Snow came home again, looking very lean and ill, but still the same dear, good-tempered cat he was before he left us. The front door being opened to allow a visitor to go out, Snow suddenly sprang in, and rushed upstairs as fast as his long legs would take him. Springing on one of our little beds, he commenced kneading the soft covering in his own old fashion, purring loudly.

Oh, what excitement there was in the house, what crowding of the children round the little bed, what hugging of the cat, what hurrying down and up stairs again with saucers of milk and meat, what joyous chattering and feeling

Cats: Poetry & Prose

of Snow's once broken tail! The poor thing appeared at times almost in danger of suffocation through affection, as he was carried from one little bed to another and another, that each of the children might in turn enjoy the cat's company.

Mrs. Surr, Pets and Playfellows

Cats: Poetry & Prose

I am the cat of cats, I am
The everlasting cat!
Cunning, and old, and sleek as jam,
The everlasting cat!
I hunt the vermin in the night –
The everlasting cat!
For I see best without the light –
The everlasting cat!

William Brightly Rands, The Cat of Cats

Cats: Poetry & Prose

If man could be crossed with the cat it would improve man, but it would deteriorate the cat.

Mark Twain

The trouble with a kitten is that eventually it becomes a cat.

Ogden Nash, "The Kitten" Verses

Cats: Poetry & Prose

I would never wound a cat's feelings, no
matter how downright aggressive I might be
to humans.

A L Rowse, Three Cornish Cats

What cats most appreciate in a human
being is not the ability to produce food
which they take for granted but his or her
entertainment value.

Geoffrey Househould

Cats: Poetry & Prose

Sam raised his paw for all the world as if he were about to protest, and then, apparently thinking better of it, he pretended instead that the action had been only for the purpose of commencing his nightly wash.

Walter de la Mare

Cats: Poetry & Prose

Hear and attend and listen; for this befell
and behappened and became and was,
O my best beloved, when the Tame
animals were wild.

The Dog was wild, and the Horse was wild,
and the Cow was wild, and the Sheep was
wild, and the Pig was wild – as wild as wild
could be – and they walked in the Wet Wild
Woods by their wild lones. But the wildest of
all the wild animals was the Cat. He walked
by himself, and all places were alike to him.

*Rudyard Kipling, The Cat that Walked by
Himself, from the Just So Stories*

Cats: Poetry & Prose

A cat that lives with a good family is used to being talked to all the time.

Lettice Cooper

You always ought to have tom cats arranged, you know – it makes 'em more companionable.

Noel Coward

Cats: Poetry & Prose

When the tea is brought at five o'clock,
And all the neat curtains are drawn with
 care,
The little black cat with bright green eyes,
Is suddenly purring there.

At first she pretends, having nothing to do,
She has come in merely to blink by the grate,
But though tea may be late or the milk may
 be sour
She is never late.

Harold Monro, Milk for the Cat

Cats: Poetry & Prose

I think one reason we admire cats,
those of us who do, is their proficiency in
one-upmanship. They always seem to come
out on top, no matter what they are doing –
or pretend they do.

Rarely do you see a cat discomfited.
They have no conscience, and they never
regret. Maybe we secretly envy them.

Barbara Webster

Cats: Poetry & Prose

He blinks upon the hearth-rug
And yawns in deep content,
Accepting all the comforts
That Providence has sent.

Louder he purrs and louder,
In one glad hymn of praise
For all the night's adventures,
For quiet, restful days.

Life will go on forever,
With all that cat can wish,
Warmth, and the glad procession
Of fish and milk and fish.

Cats: Poetry & Prose

Only the thought disturbs him –
He's noticed once or twice,
That times are somehow breeding
A nimbler race of mice.

Sir Alexander Gray, On a Cat Aging

Cats: Poetry & Prose

What female heart can gold despise?
What cat's averse to fish?

Thomas Gray,
Ode on the Death of a Favourite Cat

If a fish is the movement of water embodied,
given shape, then a cat is a diagram and
pattern of subtle air.

Doris Lessing

Cats: Poetry & Prose

It was soon noticed that when there was work to be done the cat could never be found.

George Orwell, Animal Farm

I have just been given a very engaging Persian Kitten . . . and his opinion is that I have been given to him.

Evelyn Underhill

Cats: Poetry & Prose

The cat sees through shut lids.

English Proverb

Cats are rather delicate creatures and they
are subject to a good many different
ailments, but I never heard of one who
suffered from insomnia.

Joseph Wood Krutch

Cats: Poetry & Prose

I shall never forget the indulgence with which he [Dr Johnson] treated Hodge, his cat; for whom he used to go out and buy oysters, lest the servants having that trouble should take a dislike to the poor creature.

I am, unluckily, one of those who have an antipathy to a cat, so I am uneasy when in the room with one; and I own, I frequently suffered a good deal from the presence of the same Hodge. I recollect him scrambling up Dr. Johnson's breast, apparently with much satisfaction, while my friend, half smiling and half whistling, rubbed down his back and pulled him by the tail.

Cats: Poetry & Prose

And when I observed he was a fine cat,
saying, 'why yes, Sir, but I have had cats
whom I liked better than this'; and then,
as if perceiving Hodge to be out of
countenance, adding, 'but he is a very fine
cat, a very fine cat indeed.'

James Boswell, Boswell's Life of Johnson

Cats: Poetry & Prose

Pussy will rub my knees with her head
Pretending she loves me hard;
But the very minute I go to bed
Pussy runs out in the yard.

Rudyard Kipling

Cats: Poetry & Prose

Cats are among the most grateful of dumb
creatures. The slightest attention shown
them, in the way of a kindly stroke of
their soft fur, is quite sufficient to set
them purring with joyful gratitude.
We have known cats that were suffering
intense pain stay their piteous cries,
when we rubbed their heads, to sing
us a thankful song.

Few sick human beings are able thus to
forget their sufferings when they feel the
touch of a friend's hand or hear the sound
of a sympathizing voice. Many endure a
serious illness with great patience, but few

Cats: Poetry & Prose

are able to show themselves so superior to pain that they can sing while they suffer.

Mrs. Surr, Pets and Playfellows

Cats: Poetry & Prose

Let take a cat, and foster him well with milk
And tender meat and make his couch of silk,
But let him see a mouse go by the wall,
He will abandon milk and meat and all,
And every dainty that is in that house,
Such is his appetite to eat a mouse.

Geoffrey Chaucer, The Canterbury Tales

Cats: Poetry & Prose

. . . you are my cat and I am your human.

Hilaire Belloc

A kitten is so flexible that she is almost double, the hind parts are equivalent to another kitten with which the forepart plays. She does not discover that her tail belongs to her until you tread on it.

Henry David Thoreau

Cats: Poetry & Prose

The cat loves fish, but hates wet feet.

Italian Proverb

Do you see that kitten chasing so prettily her own tail? If you could look with her eyes, you might see her surrounded with hundreds of figures performing complex dramas, with tragic and comic issues, long conversations, many ups and downs of fate.

Ralph Waldo Emerson

Cats: Poetry & Prose

Alice went on,

"And how do you know that you're mad?"

"To begin with," said the Cat, "a dog's not mad. You grant that?"

"I suppose so," said Alice.

"Well, then," the Cat went on, "You see a dog growls when it's angry, and wags its tail when it's pleased. Now I growl when I'm pleased and wag my tail when I'm angry. Therefore I'm mad."

Cats: Poetry & Prose

"I call it purring, not growling," said Alice.

"Call it what you like," said the Cat.

Lewis Carroll, Alice in Wonderland

Cats: Poetry & Prose

Cats must have three names – an everyday name, such as Peter; a more particular, dignified name, such as Quaxo, Bombalurina, or Jellylorum, and, thirdly, the name the cat thinks up for himself, his deep and inscrutable singular Name.

T S Eliot

Cats: Poetry & Prose

Now puss, while folks are in their beds,
   treads leads,
And sleepers, waking grumble – 'Drat that
   cat!'
Who in the gutter caterwauls, squalls, mauls
Some feline foe, and screams in shrill ill will.

Hood, A Nocturnal Sketch

Cats: Poetry & Prose

Confront a child, a puppy, and a kitten
with sudden danger; the child will turn
instinctively for assistance, the puppy will
grovel in abject submission to the impending
visitation, the kitten will brace its tiny body
for a frantic resistance.

Saki

Cats: Poetry & Prose

He seems the incarnation of everything soft and silky and velvety, without a sharp edge in his composition, a dreamer whose philosophy is sleep and let sleep.

Saki

Odd things animals.
All dogs look up to you.
All cats look down to you.
Only a pig looks at you as an equal.

Winston Churchill

Cats: Poetry & Prose

She sights a Bird – she chuckles
She flattens – then she crawls
She runs without the look of feet
Her eyes increase to Balls.

Emily Dickinson

Cats: Poetry & Prose

The dog wakes three times to watch
over his master; the cat wakes three times
to strangle him.

French Proverb

If we treated everyone we meet with the
same affection we bestow upon our favourite
cat, they, too would purr.

Martin Buxbaum

Cats: Poetry & Prose

A cat has absolute emotional honesty: human beings, for one reason or another, may hide their feelings, but a cat does not.

Ernest Hemingway

A man has to work so hard that something of his personality stays alive. A tomcat has it so easy, he has only to spray and his presence is there for years on rainy days.

Albert Einstein

Cats: Poetry & Prose

Dearest cat, honoured guest of my old house,
Arch your supple, tingling back,
And curl upon my knee, to let me
Bathe my fingers in your warm fur.

François Lemaitre

Cats: Poetry & Prose

That way look, my Infant, lo!
What a pretty baby-show!
See the Kitten on the wall,
Sporting with the leaves that fall,
Withered leaves—one—two—and three—
From the lofty elder-tree!
Through the calm and frosty air
Of this morning bright and fair.
Eddying round and round they sink,
Softly, slowly: one might think,
From the motions that are made,
Every little leaf conveyed
Sylph or Fairy hither tending,—
To his lower world descending,
Each invisible and mute,
In this wavering parachute.

Cats: Poetry & Prose

But the Kitten, how she starts,
Crouches, stretches, paws and darts;
First at one, and then its fellow
Just as light and just as yellow;
There are many now—now one—
Now they stop, and there are none—
What intenseness of desire
In her upward eye of fire!
With a tiger-leap half way
Now she meets her coming prey,
Lets it go as fast, and then
Has it in her power again.
Now she works with three and four,
Like an Indian conjuror;
Quick as he in feats of art,
Far beyond in joy of heart.

Cats: Poetry & Prose

Were her antics played in the eye
Of a thousand standers-by,
Clapping hands with shout and stare,
What would little Tabby care?
For the plaudits of the crowd?
Over happy to be proud,
Over wealthy in the treasure
Of her own exceeding pleasure!

William Wordsworth, The Kitten and the Falling Leaves

Cats: Poetry & Prose

We should be careful to get out of an experience only the wisdom that is in it and stop there, lest we be like the cat that sits on a hot stove lid. She will never sit down on a hot stove lid again and that is well; but also she will never sit down on a cold one any more.

Mark Twain

Cats: Poetry & Prose

A home without a cat – and a well-fed, well-petted and properly revered cat – may be a perfect home, perhaps, but how can it prove its title?

Mark Twain

'A cat may look at a king,' said Alice.

Lewis Carroll, Alice in Wonderland

Cats: Poetry & Prose

I have just been called to the door by the
sweet voice of Toss, whose morning
proceedings are wonderful. . . .
she comes to my door and gives a mew,
and then – especially if I let her in,
and go on writing or reading without taking
any notice of her – there is a real
demonstration of affection, such as never
again occurs in the day. She purrs, she walks
round and round me, she jumps in my lap,
she turns to me and rubs her head
and nose against my chin, she opens her
mouth and raps her pretty white teeth
against my pen.

Cats: Poetry & Prose

Then she leaps down, settles herself
by the fire, and never shows any more
affection all day.

Matthew Arnold

Cats: Poetry & Prose

There wanst was two cats of Kilkenny.
And aich thought there was wan cat
   too many,
So they quarrelled and fit,
And they scratched and they bit,
Till barrin' their nails and the tips of
   their tails,
Instead of two cats, there warn't any.

Anonymous

Cats: Poetry & Prose

The cat lives alone, has no need of society,
obeys only when she pleases, pretends
to sleep that she may see the more clearly,
and scratches everything on which
she can lay her paw.

François René de Chateaubriand

When a cat adopts you there is nothing to be
done about it except to put up with it and
wait until the wind changes.

T S Eliot

Cats: Poetry & Prose

Jellicle Cats are black and white,
Jellicle Cats are rather small;
Jellicle Cats are merry and bright,
And pleasant to hear when they caterwaul.
Jellicle Cats have cheerful faces,
Jellicle Cats have bright black eyes;
They like to practise their airs and graces
And wait for the Jellicle Moon to rise.

T S Eliot, The Song of the Jellicles

Cats: Poetry & Prose

It is a very inconvenient habit of kittens (Alice had once made the remark) that, whatever you say to them, they always purr. "If they would only purr for 'yes,' and mew for 'no,' or any rule of that sort," she had said, "so that one could keep up a conversation! But how can you talk with a person if they always say the same thing."

Lewis Carroll, Through the Looking-Glass

Cats: Poetry & Prose

Good king of cats, nothing but one of your nine lives.

William Shakespeare, Romeo & Juliet

When moving to a new home, always put the cat through the window instead of the door, so that it will not leave.

American Superstition

Cats: Poetry & Prose

Cats are everywhere at home where one feeds them.

German Proverb

Should ever anything be missed – milk, coals, umbrellas, brandy—
The cat's pitched into with a boot or anything that's handy.

C S Calverley

Cats: Poetry & Prose

If you drop Vladimir by mistake,
you know he always falls on his feet.
And if Vladimir tumbles off the roof of
the hut he always falls on his feet.
Cats always fall on their feet, on their four
paws, and never hurt themselves.

And as in tumbling, it is in life.
No cat is ever unfortunate for very long.
The worse things look for a cat,
the better they are going to be.

Arthur Ransome,
The Cat who Became Head-Forester

Cats: Poetry & Prose

You get your cat and you call him
Thomas or George, as the case may be.
So far, so good.

Then one morning you wake up and find
six kittens in the hat-box and you have
to re-open the matter, approaching it
from an entirely different angle.

P G Wodehouse

Beware of those who dislike cats.

Traditional

Cats: Poetry & Prose

A cat is a lion in a jungle of small bushes.

Indian Proverb

Cats when terrified stand at full height
and arch their backs in a well-known and
ridiculous fashion. They spit, hiss, or growl,
the hair over the whole body, and especially
on the tail, becomes erect.

Charles Darwin

Cats: Poetry & Prose

Cats can be very funny and have the oddest ways of showing they're glad to see you. Rudimac always peed in our shoes.

W H Auden

There are two means of refuge from the miseries of life: music and cats.

Albert Schweitzer

Cats: Poetry & Prose

For I will consider my Cat Jeoffry.

For he is the servant of the Living God, duly
and daily serving Him.

For at the first glance of the glory of God in
the East he worships in his way.

For this is done by wreathing body seven
times round with elegant quickness,

For then he leaps up to catch the musk,
which is the blessing of God upon his
prayer.

For he rolls upon prank to work it in.

For having done duty and received blessing
he begins to consider himself.

For this he performs in ten degrees.

Cats: Poetry & Prose

For first he looks upon his fore-paws to see if
    they are clean.
For secondly he kicks up behind to clear
    away there.
For thirdly he works it upon stretch with the
    fore-paws extended.
For forthly he sharpens his paws by wood.
For fifthly he washes himself.
For sixthly he rolls upon wash.
For seventhly he fleas himself, that he may
    not be interrupted upon the beat.
For eighthly he rubs himself against a post.
For ninthly he looks up for his instructions.
For tenthly he goes in quest of food.
. . .

Cats: Poetry & Prose

For he is of the tribe of Tiger.

For the Cherub Cat is a term of the Angel
  Tiger.

For he has the subtlety and hissing of a
  serpent, which in goodness he suppresses.

For he will not do destruction, if he is well-
  fed, neither will he spit without
  provocation.

For he purrs in thankfulness, when God tells
  him he's a good Cat.

For he is an instrument for the children to
  learn benevolence upon.

For every house is incomplete without him
  and a blessing is lacking in the spirit.

Christopher Smart, Jubilate Agno

Cats: Poetry & Prose

All cats love a cushioned couch.

Theocritus

I am as vigilant as a cat to steal cream.

William Shakespeare, Henry IV

One cat leads to another.

Ernest Hemingway

Cats: Poetry & Prose

The way Dinah washed her children's faces was this: first she held the poor thing down by its ear with one paw, and then with the other paw she rubbed its face all over, the wrong way, beginning at the nose: and just now, as I said, she was hard at work on the white kitten, which was lying quite still and trying to purr – no doubt feeling that it was all meant for its good.

Lewis Carroll, Through the Looking-Glass

Cats: Poetry & Prose

And let me touch those curving claws of yellow ivory, and grasp the tail that like a monstrous asp coils round your heavy velvet paws.

Oscar Wilde

Cats like men, are flatterers.

Walter Savage Landor

Cats: Poetry & Prose

Old cats mean young mice.

Italian Proverb

It is called in Hebrew Catul;
    in Chaldean Chatul, pl. Chatulin;
    in Greek Katus; in Latin Catus or felis;
    in English the Cat.

William Salmon

Cats: Poetry & Prose

A cat belonging to M Piccini has assured us,
that they who only know how to mew, cannot
be any judges of the art of singing.

Benjamin Franklin

The ideal of calm exists in a sitting cat.

Jules Reynard

Cats: Poetry & Prose

In a cat's eyes, all things belong to cats.

English Proverb

A scalded cat dreads even cold water.

French Proverb

A bashful cat makes a proud mouse.

Scottish Proverb

Cats: Poetry & Prose

He that denies the cat skimmed milk must give the mouse cream.

Russian Proverb

All animals are equal, but some animals are more equal than others.

George Orwell, Animal Farm

Cats: Poetry & Prose

Cat! who hast pass'd thy grand climacteric,
How many mice and rats hast in thy days
Destroy'd? – How many titbits stolen? Gaze
With those bright languid segments green,
   and prick
Those velvet ears – but pr'ythee do not stick
Thy latent talons in me – and upraise
Thy gentle mew – and tell me all thy frays
Of fish and mice, and rats and tender chick.
Nay, look not down, nor lick thy dainty wrists –
For all the wheezy asthma, – and for all
Thy tail's tip is nick'd off – and though the
   fists
Of many a maid have given thee many a
   maul,

Cats: Poetry & Prose

Still is that fur as soft as when the lists
In youth thou enter'dst on glass bottled wall.

John Keats, Sonnet to Mrs Reynolds' Cat

Cats: Poetry & Prose

It is lost labour to play a jig to an old cat.

Thomas Fuller

When the cat's away the mice will play.

Traditional

To err is human
To purr feline

Robert Byrne

Acknowledgements:

Kittens at Play by Leon Charles Huber (1858-1928)
Haynes Fine Art/Fine Art Photographs

Kittens Playing with Pearls Marie-Yvonne Laur (b.1879)
Private Collection/Fine Art Photographs

Family Fun by Alfred Arthur Brunel de Neuville (1852-1941)
Cox & Co./Fine Art Photographs

Mischief Makers by Henriette Ronner-Knip (1821-1909)
Fine Art of Oakham/Fine Art Photographs

A Balancing Act by Leon Charles Huber (1858-1928)
Gavin Graham Gallery/Fine Art Photographs

"Own-Up" by Leon Charles Huber (1858-1928)
Burlington Paintings/Fine Art Photographs